MARMION
the MARSHMALLOW

Story and Illustrations
by Marie Chu

This book is made possible by Mom and Baba.

ISBN-13: 978-0615783932

Someone left the cupboard door
O P E N !

Marmion, a marshmallow, had been sitting in the dark for a long time. He felt stuck in the plastic bag with all the other marshmallows. He slipped out of the bag, walked to the open door, and looked outside.

The other marshmallows yelled, "Don't go! It's not safe!"

But Marmion wanted to go outside. He felt BRAVE. He climbed down to the countertop.

The world outside was huge, and so different from the cupboard. It was very, very **bright**. The countertop seemed to go on forever. The ceiling towered HIGH above. The world seemed... a little scary.

Marmion soon met a red and round apple who was on the counter. His name was Harold.

"Hello!" Harold said. "Why are you all alone and wandering outside your plastic bag?"

"Does everyone outside have a skin to protect them?" he asked.

"I don't know," Harold said. "But, everyone I know has one!"

"I want to see the world outside the cupboard," Marmion said. He looked at Harold and said, "Aren't you outside alone too?"

"Oh, yes," Harold agreed. "But I have a skin to protect me."

Marmion thought, "I don't have a skin."

Marmion wondered, "Should I be walking all alone outside without a skin?"

Marmion met Betty, a friend of Harold's. She was a banana.

"I have a skin." she said. "A thick skin!"

Betty looked down the counter and said, "Hey, here comes Penny! She's a pistachio nut."

Harold said, "Carl! What are you doing outside your candy jar? Marmion, this is Carl, he's a chocolate candy."

Marmion asked Penny if she had a skin too.

"Hi, Marmion!" Penny said. "I have a shell on the outside, instead of skin. A shell's a lot harder and tougher than a skin. Carl has a shell too."

"That's right!" Carl said, knocking his hand on his shell.

Marmion wanted to be tough too. He worried even more as he walked down the countertop.

But then, he saw a box of plastic wrap on the counter, and had an idea. "I will make a plastic bag just for me!"

Marmion wrapped, and he rolled the plastic around and around.

Marmion finished wrapping and rolling. "I can't see very well. It's hard to breathe. And it's hard to move. This plastic wrap is a bad idea!"

Carl came over to help unwrap the plastic from Marmion.

"What should I do, Carl?" Marmion asked. "I'm a marshmallow, and I'm soft. I don't have a skin or shell to protect me."

"I know!" Carl said. "There's a special chocolate sauce. It makes a shell when you pour it out."

This sounded like a great idea. "I'll try it!" Marmion said. "I'm happy my new friends are so helpful."

After waiting several minutes, Marmion had a chocolate shell. He felt BRAVER. "I'm tough now!" Marmion said. "Oh, but the chocolate tickles my nose..."

OOPS.

Marmion decided to try and make a shell from something else. He ran to the sugar bowl and said, "Carl, pour some sugar out! I'll roll in the sugar. It may tickle, but this time, the sugar WILL STICK."

Now Marmion had a skin made of sugar. But, ... he heard a *buzzing* sound.

"Oh no! Bees like the sugar!" Carl said.

Marmion ran and ran really, really fast. He brushed the sugar off while he ran.

Marmion looked behind to see if the bee was still following him.
He didn't see where he was going.

"It's a good thing I'm too soft to knock any of those books over."

But he was wrong.

CRASH!

Marmion heard footsteps. His new friends heard the CRASH of the book.

"Do you need some help Marmion?" they asked.

"Yes, please!" Marmion said.

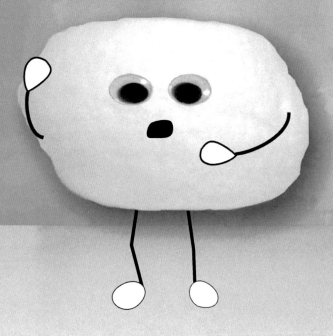

Marmion got up and pushed himself back into shape.

"I'm glad I'm soft enough to get smooshed!" he said.

"Hurray!" everyone shouted, "It's a good thing you're a marshmallow!"

"I love being soft!" Marmion said.

The End

Made in the USA
Las Vegas, NV
11 October 2021